understanding
buddy

understanding
buddy

Marc Kornblatt

MARGARET K. McELDERRY BOOKS
New York London Toronto Sydney Singapore

Margaret K. McElderry Books
An imprint of Simon & Schuster Children's Publishing Division
1230 Avenue of the Americas
New York, NY 10020

Book design by Sonia Chaghatzbanian
The text of this book is set in Horley Old Style.
Printed in the United States of America
2 4 6 8 10 9 7 5 3 1

Library of Congress Cataloging-in-Publication Data
Kornblatt, Marc.
Understanding Buddy / by Marc Kornblatt.—1st ed.
p. cm.
Summary: When a new classmate stops speaking because of the
sudden death of his mother, fifth-grader Sam tries to befriend him and
risks destroying his relationship with his best friend, Alex.
ISBN 0-689-83215-X
[1. Death—Fiction. 2. Grief—Fiction. 3. Mutism, Elective—Fiction. 4.
Schools—Fiction. 5. Friendship—Fiction. 6. Jews—United States—
Fiction.] I. Title.
PZ7.K8373 Sh 2000
[Fic]-dc21
99-046913

For
Jacob, Louisa,
and Paula

understanding
buddy

tonight at supper Martha asked Dad what he thought happened to the deer Laura White hit the day she died. Dad gave her a weird look, like the face Charlie Chaplin makes in the movie *Modern Times* when he eats a bowl of hot cereal seasoned with sneezing powder. Except Charlie's face is funny, and Dad's wasn't.

"How did you know Laura died?" he asked.

"I just knew," Martha said.

"Did you hear Mommy and me talking about her?"

"No."

"Then who told you?" Dad looked straight at me. "Did Sam?"

I thought Martha was going to tattletale. I stopped chewing my spaghetti and held my breath.

"No, Daddy," she said. "A little birdie did."

Dad smiled. I started breathing again. That Martha. For a six-year-old kid who can barely read, she says some pretty cool things once in a while. Of course, I'd never tell her that. It would just go to her head, which is already big enough, thanks to Mom and Dad always saying how cute she is.

The only reason I told Martha about Laura's death in the first place was because she wanted to play with the controls in Mom's car. I tried to explain to her how fooling around like that could release the parking brake, and the car might start rolling down the driveway. That got me on to the subject of car accidents, and before I knew it I had told her about Laura.

I didn't mean to do it. Dad had told me what happened, man to man. That means I was supposed to understand Martha is too young to hear that kind of stuff, but it just slipped out.

Laura has been on my mind a lot lately. She

was a big, smiley woman with muddy brown hair and a lumpy face who used to be our cleaning lady. I admit, I wasn't crazy about her when she first came to work for us. One reason was I didn't want a stranger poking around in my room, even if she *was* there to get rid of the dust bunnies. I was afraid she would knock over one of my model skyscrapers, or mess up the South American beetle collection on my shelf, or rearrange the personal things in one of my drawers.

Another reason I wasn't crazy about her at the beginning was her personality. A stranger stays a stranger with me for a while before I start acting friendly. That first day Laura showed up at our house, she acted the exact opposite. I was trying to get ready for school, putting my lunch in my backpack, when the bell rang. I could have gone out through the kitchen and let Mom open the front door, but I thought I'd do her a favor.

Laura waddled in like a bear and held out her huge, red hand for me to shake.

"Who might you be?" she asked with a big smile.

"Sam," I said.

"And what grade are you in, Sammy?"

"Fourth."

"Well, what do you know about that? My Buddy's in fourth grade, too." I nodded as politely as I could and said, "I have to go to school now."

Laura winked at me like we shared some important secret.

"Have a great day, Sammy," she said, patting me on the head.

The pat on the head really annoyed me.

Laura only came to clean twice a month, and every time I saw her she gave me the same big smile, the same big handshake, the same wink and pat on the head. After a while I got used to her hellos, just like I got used to her calling me Sammy instead of Sam, because I could tell she was just trying to be nice. She also called Martha Marty, Mom Sandy, and Dad Bobby. I had never heard anybody call my dad Bobby before, which was one of the things I liked about Laura.

After saying hello, she almost always had something to ask.

"Tell me, Sammy," she said one of the first times. "How are you at long division?"

"Okay," I answered. "I got an 84 on my last quiz."

Laura nodded. "Do you like doing your homework?"

"No."

"Same with my Buddy."

She asked me about my friends and about sports and about so many other things that after a while we stopped being strangers. The last time I ran into her on my way out of the house, Laura gave me one of her usual big hellos and asked me what I was doing for summer vacation. "Swim team, a typing course, hanging around the house," I told her. "And a family camping trip."

"That sounds very nice." She patted my head and looked at me like she was measuring me for a sweater. "You're a nice boy, Sammy," she said. "Nice boys deserve to have nice summers."

Then she waddled up the front steps and disappeared into our house.

I didn't think much about it then, but after she died I kept hearing Laura's voice in my head. I missed her big hellos and having her call me Sammy. And I found myself thinking about where she was, wondering if she had a soul that climbed up a ladder to heaven like the one Jacob from the Bible saw in his dreams, or if all that was left of her was a dead body lying in the ground.

Dad told me that Laura was on her way to work for a family that lived near Leopold Forest when she smashed into a tree. It was a drizzly morning, and the streets were slippery. The police think her car skidded off the road when she swerved to avoid running over a deer. They know she grazed a deer at least, because they found blood and fur splattered along the edge of the car's front bumper. But they never found the deer.

When I asked Dad what he thought happened to Laura after she died he said, "Well, I know her body is buried in the cemetery."

"What about her soul?"

"I can't tell you where her soul is."

"What about heaven?"

"If there's a heaven, then maybe it's there."

"What do you mean *if*?"

"I mean, I don't know. Our people don't think about heaven much."

"Why not?"

"Because we're too busy living this life."

I wasn't sure what Dad meant exactly, but I didn't ask him to explain, because I thought I'd only get more confused. So I dropped the subject.

Dad made me promise to keep our discussion to myself. He said it was confidential. I kept my promise for 73 days, up until this afternoon.

I'm hoping Dad will forget about Martha's deer question before Mom comes home from her business trip, though I probably shouldn't worry. I think he wasn't supposed to tell me about Laura, either. The only thing Mom told me was that Laura wouldn't be working for us anymore.

Whether Dad does or doesn't forget, I know I shouldn't have told Martha about Laura's death. Now she'll probably have nightmares, and it will be my fault. But I couldn't help it. Laura has been floating around in my thoughts a lot lately, and today something happened that almost brought her back from the dead.

It was the first day of school, and a new kid, someone I never saw at Farmdale Elementary before, walked into my fifth-grade class and sat at a desk three seats behind me. His name is Buddy White.

i tried to talk to Buddy at recess today.

"My name is Sam," I said. "Sam Keeperman."

Buddy stared at me without saying a word for so long that I got embarrassed holding out my hand and let it drop. I wanted to tell him I was sorry about his mom. I wanted to tell him how she used to call my dad Bobby. I wanted to tell him all kinds of other things about her to help him feel better, but the look in his eyes told me to stop before I had even started. After that, he turned and walked into the school building.

I couldn't figure out if he recognized my name or not. I still can't, because I didn't try to talk to him again. The problem is, I don't know what to say. How do you start a conversation with a kid who lost his mom three months ago when he won't even say hello? I can't even imagine what it would be like to lose mine. Just thinking about it gives me a stomachache.

Buddy doesn't look at all like Laura. For one thing, he's short. The top of his head barely reaches my chin. For another thing, he's skinny and has bad posture. Laura used to stand with her shoulders back, but Buddy walks hunched over like someone caught in the rain. His hair and skin are a lot darker than hers, too. But that doesn't matter. Even if he never smiled I would still know he's her son. The reason I know it is because he came to school today wearing a tie-dye shirt with the words SAN FRANCISCO IS A GIANT TOWN on the front. My aunt Maddy is a San Francisco Giants fan. She gave me that shirt. I'm not really a tie-dye type of guy, so I wore the shirt maybe twice before it got too small for me. Mom put the shirt in a grocery bag with some other stuff that didn't fit me and gave it to Laura.

It felt weird seeing Buddy walk into class wearing my old T-shirt. I wonder if he knew it once belonged to me, though I bet he probably doesn't care. I wonder about his shoulders. Has he always walked with them hunched over, or did he start doing that after his mom died? I wonder what he thinks about his mom now. Does he believe she has a soul that is floating around in heaven, or that she's just a dead body lying in the cemetery?

I wish I didn't wonder so much about this stuff, but it's hard not to when I knew the person who died and her son sits like a zombie three desks away from me.

After school I biked home with my best friend Alex Kohler like we do almost every day. Alex thinks Buddy belongs in a special ed class.

"The kid is retarded," said Alex. "He can't even pick up a pencil."

"Just because he doesn't pick up his pencil doesn't mean he can't," I said.

"If he knows how, then why doesn't he do it?"

"How do I know?"

"Believe me, Sam, he's retarded."

Alex and I have been friends since we were

little. He lives two blocks away from me on Lincoln Street, and we do almost everything together. We met at a preschool called Pammy's Place. I don't remember anything about Pammy's, not even Alex, but Mom told me we became friends on the very first day.

For as long as I can remember knowing him, Alex has always liked to say goofy things. I usually know when to take him seriously and when not to, and most of the time I can destroy his dumb theories. But I really didn't know much about Buddy, so I had nothing to say about him and special ed. At least nothing that I wanted to share.

I'm sure Buddy is so sad that he doesn't want to say or do anything. Who wouldn't be after losing his mom? But there was no way I was going to tell Alex about Laura. Tell Alex a secret like that today, and everyone in the whole fifth grade will know about it tomorrow. And I'm not going to be the one to make Buddy stand out if what he wants is to be left alone.

Who knows? Maybe Alex is right about Buddy. He does sit next to him in class and has watched him up close for the past two days.

Maybe Buddy really does have learning problems and belongs in special ed. But if that's true, wouldn't our principal know it? When I asked Alex that he bugged his eyes at me and whispered, "Maybe Mr. Franklin is mentally retarded, too!"

Sometimes Alex can be pretty funny.

3

t oday I did two stupid things. The first stupid thing I did was follow Buddy after class instead of going straight to Hebrew school.

I know it was wrong, but I wanted to find out where Laura had lived before she died. It was the same kind of feeling I have when I want to see a sad movie. I know it's going to make my eyes burn, but I still want to see it. And Buddy made it easy, because he never looked back. I couldn't tell if he knew I was walking my bike behind him or not.

So I followed him down Washington Avenue past Dad's law office to a little shoe repair shop on a street with a bunch of houses that needed paint jobs. If Madison, Wisconsin, was a Monopoly board, Dad's office building would be on an expensive yellow-card street like Marvin Gardens. The shoe repair store would be on purple Baltic Avenue.

After Buddy went into the shoe shop, I stopped in front to get a closer look. A neon sign in the window said HEELS IN TEN MINUTES, SOLES IN AN HOUR. Inside I saw a man shining shoes at a machine with one of those round brushes that spins real fast. He never looked up from his work, so I couldn't see his face, but I'll bet the man was Buddy's dad. He had dark hair and was short and thin just like Buddy, and he hunched his shoulders to keep off invisible rain the same way Buddy does.

The second stupid thing I did today happened while I was watching Buddy's dad work. Buddy turned around and caught me staring through the window. Everything might have been fine if I had acted like I was just passing by. I could have smiled, and waved, and kept on walking. Or I might have gone into the shop to say hello. Or, maybe, Buddy might have come out and said something to me, finally.

Anyway, none of that happened, of course, because I pedaled away as fast as I could.

4

after spending all yesterday afternoon and night feeling dumb, I went up to Buddy the first thing this morning to apologize.

"I'm sorry I spied on you," I said. "It was wrong."

He just stared at me and walked away. What could he have been thinking? I have no idea.

At lunch I asked Alex if he still thought Buddy needed special ed.

"Definitely," he said. "The kid can't even tie his own tennis shoes."

"How do you know?"

"Just look at his laces."

"Other kids go around with their laces untied."

"That's because they want to. He has no other choice."

Instead of arguing, I dropped the subject and decided to ignore Buddy. Okay, I thought. If he doesn't want to even say hello, then there's nothing else I can do right now. At least I tried.

Everything was fine until I got to the park after school. My soccer team, the Farmdale Fliers, had its first practice, and we have a new player—Buddy White. And to make things worse, he came dressed in a T-shirt I used to wear all the time before it got too small. The shirt has drawings of different kinds of bird poop on the front and a Chippewa Indian eagle design on the back that I stenciled myself. Alex recognized it, of course.

"Hey, Buddy," he said. "Where did you get the cool-looking T-shirt?"

Buddy didn't answer.

Alex turned to me. "Sam, what's Buddy doing with that shirt?"

"I'll tell you later," I said. But that wasn't good enough.

"Hey, Buddy," Alex tried again. "How did you get Sam's shirt?"

Buddy looked at him like he couldn't believe what Alex had just said. It all felt like my fault.

Buddy headed for the water fountain. Alex followed him.

"How'd you get the shirt, Buddy?"

I ran after them.

"Alex!" I punched him in the arm, but he wouldn't shut up.

"Buddy, how'd you get the cool shirt?"

Then Andy Spinner joined in.

"Cool shirt, Buddy," he said. "How'd you get it?"

"Be quiet, Warthog," I told him. Andy really does look like a warthog.

"Make me." Andy oinked in my face. "Cool shirt, Buddy," he said with a laugh. "How'd you get it?"

"How'd you get it?" mimicked Kurt Paulson.

"Shut up, Lizard," I shouted. Kurt's nickname fits him perfectly, too.

They kept pestering him while Buddy leaned over the fountain and took a long drink of water.

"Cool shirt," snorted Warthog.

"How'd you get it?" hissed Lizard.

"Cool shirt."

"Cool shirt."

"Where'd you get it?"

"Where'd you get it?"

Alex stood there grinning.

"You're a jerk," I said.

"Why?"

I shook my head and tried to push Warthog away, but he wouldn't leave. Lizard wouldn't leave, either.

"Where'd you get it?"

"Where'd you get it?"

I gave Alex one of my meanest looks.

"Okay, you guys," Alex finally said. "Cut it out."

When Warthog muttered something else, Alex put him in a headlock. That shut him up and Lizard, too, but it was too late. I was really mad.

Mr. Taylor blew his whistle to start practice. He introduced Buddy and put him on the front line to see what he could do. A lot, it turned out. Even with his shoelaces untied, he ran faster than everyone. He could also dribble with both feet. No one could stop him, not even Alex, who is our best player. At the end of practice Mr. Taylor gave Buddy a thumbs-up and called him a natural.

Buddy didn't say thank you. He left without even waving good-bye.

"So, what was he doing with your bird poop T-shirt?" Alex asked me again.

"Why should I tell you?" I got on my bike and rode away.

Alex caught up with me after a block.

"What are you so mad about?"

"What do you think?"

"Sorry. I didn't expect Lizard and Warthog to butt in like that."

"That's no excuse."

"I said I'm sorry, okay?"

"Anyone who can play soccer like Buddy does not belong in special ed," I said.

"Fine. He's brilliant. Now how did he get your shirt?"

"His mother used to clean our house."

"So?"

"So, one time my mom gave her some stuff that was too small for me, like the T-shirt."

"Oh."

Alex didn't ask anything after that, and I couldn't tell if he thought it was a good thing for me to give my bird poop shirt to Laura or a bad thing. What I could tell was that he knew I was keeping something from him.

I know it was wrong to treat my best friend like that, and I feel bad about it, but after the way Alex acted at practice I also think I'm doing Buddy a favor, whether he knows it or not. Laura, too.

At dinner I told Mom and Dad that we have a new kid in class.

"His name is Buddy White," I said.

I thought Dad was about to say something, but he stopped when Mom gave him a look. He just asked, "Is he a nice boy?"

"I can't tell. He never talks."

"Why doesn't he talk?" asked Martha.

"I don't know."

Martha must have forgotten Laura's last name, or I'm sure she would have brought it up.

"Did he lose his voice?" she asked.

"Some children are very shy," Mom told her, then changed the subject by asking me about my homework.

After dinner, while I was clearing the table, Dad went out of his way to help me.

"Thanks," he said when we were alone in the kitchen.

"For what?"

"For not telling Mom that I told you about Laura."

"Why doesn't she want to talk about her?" I asked.

"She's trying to protect you and Martha."

"From what?"

"The world."

"How will our not talking about Laura protect us from the world?"

"I'm not sure." Dad stacked the dirty silverware in one neat pile before he said, "I think your mom's scared to talk about Laura because she thinks the same thing could happen to our family."

Then he put his hand on my shoulder and held it there for a while. I think he was scared, too.

5

Saturday is my most favorite and least favorite day. It's my most favorite day because it's the beginning of the weekend. It's my least favorite day because I have to go to synagogue with my parents.

Hardly any kids my own age ever show up to pray at Beth Shalom Synagogue, because it's so boring. Dad makes me read the Hebrew with him in the prayer book. Then he sends me downstairs to join the Bar and Bat Mitzvah students. I'm two years away from my Bar Mitzvah, and I already go to Hebrew school Monday and Wednesday afternoons after regular school, but Dad doesn't care. He thinks my hanging around sixth- and seventh-graders is good for my character.

The Bar and Bat Mitzvah students study the Bible and learn prayers with Mr. Nadler. Mr. Nadler is nicer than Mrs. Sherman, my Hebrew teacher, but his class is almost as boring as being upstairs with the adults. Except this morning it wasn't.

This morning we studied the story of the flood, and people talked about God's big mistake. Maybe all the humans on earth besides Noah and his family really were evil and deserved to be punished. But what about the animals? They didn't know the difference between good and bad, and they all drowned in the flood anyway, except for two of each species. How could God do that?

"I don't know," said Mr. Nadler. "The best answer I can offer is that the Lord works in mysterious ways."

I never talk in front of the older kids, but this time I couldn't help myself. Without raising my hand or anything, I said, "I think a God who kills innocent animals is no better than the people he destroyed."

Nodding heads turned my way.

"Sam is right," said Josh Klickstein, one of the class leaders. "And God was wrong."

"I totally agree," said Naomi Shrager.

Naomi gave me a smile with her perfect teeth, and I felt my face get hot. I'm sure it turned the shade of beet-colored horseradish. Everybody had something to say after that, except me. Naomi's smile gave me such a bad attack of shyness that I didn't say another word for the rest of the class.

6

martha went shopping with Mom today and came home with a long blond wig, a checked miniskirt, and little-girl high heels.

"I'm going to be Barbie for Halloween," she told me.

"What?" I asked.

"I want to be Barbie."

"Why?"

"Because she's special."

"You mean you actually *like* her?"

"Yep."

"Mom," I said, "Do you think Barbie is special?"

Mom was sticking tiny sparkly heart and flower decals to Martha's fingernails.

"If Martha thinks she's special, that's good enough for me," she said.

I shook my head. "Martha, I could see you as Wonder Woman or Supergirl. But Barbie?"

"Why not?" Martha's eyes were shiny, like she was about to cry.

Mom stopped working on the decals and waited to hear what I was going to say next. I could feel a bad storm closing in fast.

"You're right, Martha," I said, like a good big brother. "Barbie *is* special."

"More special than Supergirl and Wonder Woman?" asked Martha.

"Definitely."

"Twice as special," agreed Mom.

The storm passed, Mom went back to the decals, and I escaped to my room to play Boomerang on my computer.

I don't get it. Martha has heard me make fun of Barbie commercials plenty of times. Mom and Dad have both told her that she doesn't need to have long legs and straight blond hair to be beautiful, that it's okay to have brown curls and be a little chubby. But she still wanted to be Barbie. And that wasn't the worst part.

After her nails were all decorated, she put on her costume and rushed into my room without knocking.

"Sam," she said. "I have a great idea."

"Let's hear."

"How about if we go trick-or-treating together? You could be Ken."

"What?"

"It would be really special. And people would give us lots and lots of candy because we'd be so cute."

That Martha. I admit she looked pretty in her Barbie outfit with those hearts and flowers sparkling on her fingernails, but me dressing up as Ken? Please!

"I'll think about it," I told her.

"Yes!" she screamed, and was gone.

The truth is, I don't know what I want to be for Halloween. I have already been a puppy, a banana, a triceratops, Peter Pan, an astronaut, a werewolf, the Grim Reaper, Charlie Chaplin, and a bottle of aspirin. I think I may be getting too old for costumes, but I still like getting the candy, so I guess I'll have to play along.

Last year around Hanukkah and Christmas,

Laura wouldn't accept a holiday present from our family because she said she was a Jehovah's Witness. She told Mom that Jehovah's Witnesses don't celebrate any holidays, not even Halloween. She said that they believe that all modern holidays and celebrations, including birthdays, have pagan roots and dishonor God.

I looked up the word "pagan" in the dictionary. It means someone who is not a Christian, Muslim, or a Jew. But the dictionary didn't explain how celebrating a harmless thing like someone's birthday dishonors God. Laura probably meant that people get so carried away with stuff like presents and candy that they forget the reason they're celebrating in the first place. That makes sense to me.

Anyway, I remember when I was younger how hard it was not to celebrate Christmas like everyone else. I understood we didn't celebrate it because we weren't Christian, but that didn't make it any easier. At least I have always been allowed to go trick-or-treating. Buddy can't even do that. Or maybe he can. Maybe he's allowed to go out on Halloween the same as me so he won't feel totally left out. But I bet that right now he doesn't care about celebrating any-thing.

One of the things I have always loved about Halloween is coming home with my bag full of candy and dumping it on the dining room table. Then Mom helps me separate it into different piles for chocolates, chewies, suckers, and gum, while Dad tries to steal whatever he can when I'm not looking. If I lost one of my parents, Halloween would never be the same.

alex is wrong. Buddy doesn't need to be in special ed. I do. At recess today I asked Buddy what he was going to be for Halloween. As usual, all he did was stare at me.

"I'm just trying to be friendly," I said.

Believe it or not, I was about to invite him to go trick-or-treating with me and Alex, if his father would let him. Boy, what a dumb idea.

"Can't you answer a simple question?" I asked, getting annoyed.

No answer.

"Buddy, did you hear me?"

He turned to go.

"Buddy?" I grabbed his shoulder before he could walk away.

His answer came back so fast that I didn't have time to blink. Next thing I know there was blood trickling out of my nose. I don't care how short and skinny he is, Buddy has a hard fist. That made me even angrier.

Locking both of my arms around his head, I tried to yank him off of his feet. Buddy's elbow caught me in the stomach, but I held on tight and dragged him down with me. Kids cheered while we wrestled on the ground.

I squeezed Buddy as hard as I could and kept squeezing until I felt someone pull me from behind.

"Come on, Sam." It was Alex. "Let go of him."

"He punched me in the face!"

"You're crushing him."

Buddy's face was pale by the time I let him up. Ms. Bobson sent us to Mr. Franklin's office.

Mr. Franklin invited Buddy and me to sit in the hard blue plastic chairs in front of his desk. He looked back and forth at us for a long time. It was my first visit to the principal's office for bad behavior, and I was afraid I was going to cry while I waited for him to say something.

"Would either of you care to explain what happened?" Mr. Franklin asked finally.

He turned toward Buddy. "Mr. White?"

Buddy just stared. Mr. Franklin's eyes locked onto mine.

"Mr. Keeperman?"

I cleared my throat and tried to speak clearly, but I was sure he could hear the tears in my voice.

"It was my fault."

"Yes?"

"I used my hands when I should have used words."

"I see."

Mr. Franklin leaned back in his chair and stared at the ceiling. I looked out of the corner of my eye to see what Buddy was doing. He was as quiet as the air.

"I'll tell you what I'm going to do," Mr. Franklin said. "Since neither of you has a record of misconduct in this school, I'm going to let you both off with a warning. But if anything like this happens again, there will be serious consequences. Is that clear?"

I nodded. I didn't look to see what Buddy did. By then I didn't care. He let me take the entire blame for our fight when it was just as much his fault as it was mine, maybe even more. When am I going to learn to mind my own business?

My nose was swollen by the time I got home. The dried blood inside my left nostril felt all crusty. As soon as Martha saw me she started playing 20 Questions.

"What happened to you?" she began.

"I fell off the jungle gym at recess," I lied.

"Did someone push you?"

"No, I slipped."

"Did you cry?"

"No."

"Did you go to the nurse's office?"

"No."

"Why not?"

"Because I didn't need to go."

"Does it hurt?"

"A little."

"Why don't you put ice on it?"

"I will as soon as you stop your investigation, Miss Motor Mouth."

"What's an investigation?"

"Exactly what you're doing."

"What am I doing?"

"Martha!"

Yelling at her made my nose sting, but at least she stopped bothering me after that. Later at dinner her investigation came in handy. Little Miss Motor Mouth answered all of my parents' questions. That saved me from having to lie for the second time on the same day.

At synagogue this morning everyone in the Bar and Bat Mitzvah class wanted to know what happened to me. The spot where Buddy punched me stood out on my face like a black, blue, and yellow graffiti painting. Even Mr. Nadler was interested in hearing my story.

I wanted to tell them everything. I wanted to tell them about the fight and about Buddy's silence and about Laura's car accident. And I wanted to ask them what they thought happened to her after she died and what they would do if their moms died. But I could feel Naomi Shrager watching me, and that made me not want to say anything. So I told them I slipped in the shower.

I n school today Ms. Bobson asked us what we thought life would be like twenty years from now. We wrote a list on the board of all the different things that might happen.

The list was four columns long. It included inventions like flying cars, computers with real human brains, and a pill that will make people invisible. Some of the great events included the discovery of life on another planet, the end of disease, the end of hunger, the end of war, and the end of school. I said another great event would be the discovery of heaven. That made some people laugh, but I was serious.

Ms. Bobson said she thought the discovery of heaven was a serious subject, too. While we were talking about it, Buddy lifted his arm slowly. At first, most of the class didn't notice, but by the time his hand was all the way up, everyone saw, and we had all stopped talking.

A tear was rolling down his cheek. I watched it reach the bottom of his chin and drip onto his desk.

"Yes, Buddy?" said Ms. Bobson.

Her voice was so calm that I could tell she felt the exact opposite inside. Everyone else held still, waiting.

"Do you have a question, Buddy?" Ms. Bobson coaxed.

While we all stared, Buddy lowered his arm slowly. He sighed, shook his head, and didn't say a thing. Right then the final bell of the day rang, and we all stopped staring and got up to leave.

the Farmdale Flyers played the Wingra Wildcats today, and something amazing happened at the game. Last year the Wildcats destroyed us, 7-1, thanks to a kid named Roscoe Something-or-Other who scored five goals. Roscoe moved up to the 12-and-over league, so our teams were more even now. Plus, we had Buddy on our side.

In the first half Buddy intercepted the ball at midfield and wove in between four defenders to score a goal. The Wildcats tied the game on a penalty kick near the beginning of the second half.

For the next ten minutes the ball bounced back and forth like we were playing Ping-Pong.

It looked like the game was going to end in a tie. We were all so tired, everyone seemed to be running in slow motion.

I was playing right halfback, and my legs felt like wet cement. All I wanted to do was make sure nothing got past me. With two minutes left in the game, the Wildcats' center forward cut around Alex and booted the ball high. Lizard managed to tip it away with his head, and I outraced their wingman and got it up to Buddy. I'm not a real scorer, and I never expected Buddy would pass back to me, so I ran just fast enough to follow the play in case he lost the ball. That's when it happened.

Buddy stopped for a second, turned around, and motioned to me.

At first, I wasn't even sure what he wanted until Mr. Taylor started jumping up and down on the sidelines and screaming.

"Run up, Sam! *Run Up!*"

I sprinted as fast as I could while Buddy raced left and hit me with a perfect pass twenty feet from the goal. The pass caught the Wildcats by surprise, too. With no defenders between me and the goalkeeper, I kicked a squibbler off the side of my foot. The keeper lunged for the ball. I thought he had it for sure, but his reach was too short, and the ball slipped into the goal for the score.

Our team went crazy. People pounded my back and screamed in my ears, and everyone danced around the field. But not Buddy. He stood there like a statue when Mr. Taylor gave him a hug. He didn't even say you're welcome when I thanked him for the pass. Then his father pulled up in an old gray station wagon; Buddy got in and they drove away.

One part of me was sorry to see him go. After all, it was Buddy who really won the game for us. But another part of me was relieved. Having him around while the rest of us were celebrating was a pain.

"Well, maybe he isn't retarded," said Alex after Buddy had gone, "but he's definitely a jerk."

"No, he's not," I said.

"Then why did you have a fight with him?"

"Because . . . I was too pushy."

"You're only sticking up for him because he passed you the ball."

"No, I'm not."

Right then I should have told Alex everything I knew about Buddy and Laura, but I didn't. Maybe I was only copying my mom, but I thought it was something I should keep to myself. Besides, Alex has been so obnoxious, I didn't think he deserved to know.

"Alex," I said. "You're jealous because Buddy's a better player than you are."

"I am not." Alex shoved me.

I shoved him back, harder. "You are, too."

"Am not."

"Alex," I said, getting angry. "Now *you're* being a jerk!"

"Look who's calling who a jerk!"

Alex is two inches taller and fifteen pounds heavier than me. If he pushed with all of his might, he would have sent me flying, but I didn't give him the chance. When he tried to shove me again, I stepped aside and tripped him. Then we started fighting for real.

We both had bloody lips when Mr. Taylor separated us. He didn't care how it all started. All he said was: "Do it again and you're both off the team."

10

today I walked up to Alex and held out my hand.

"I'm sorry about what happened after the game yesterday," I said.

He just stared at my fingers like he was Buddy, then wandered away. At recess he goofed around with Lizard and Warthog. I know for a fact that he isn't really friends with Warthog, and he doesn't even like Lizard. He was goofing around with them just to bug me, so I didn't really care. But when he started making faces behind Buddy's back, I felt like hitting him again. Buddy was minding his own business. "Can't you guys leave him alone?" I said.

"Can't you guys leave him alone?" mimicked Alex.

"Can't you guys leave him alone?" copied Warthog and Lizard.

The last thing I needed was another visit to Mr. Franklin's office, so I dropped it. Alex and I didn't say a word to each other for the rest of the day.

After school, instead of biking with Alex, I went home by myself. Once I got there I had nothing else to do, so I finished my social studies report about the Brazilian rain forest. I was working on my word problems, something I almost always do with Alex, when Mom brought Martha home from her after-school tap dance class.

"Sam, what are you doing?" asked Mom, trying hard to sound shocked and amazed.

"My math homework."

"Your *what*?"

She was kidding, of course—usually I need to be reminded a couple of times to do my math homework—but I wasn't in a joking mood.

"Why are you doing your math homework?"

"Because I want to."

"Where's Alex?"

I didn't answer.

"What's wrong, Sam?"

"Nothing."

"Honey?"

I could tell she was being serious now, but I didn't feel like talking.

"Do you have a tummyache?" Martha butted in.

"No," I said. "There is nothing wrong with me. Now will you both please leave me alone?" I shut my door with a bang.

Mom must have said something to Dad, because he offered to take me down to Video Mart after dinner and let me rent anything I wanted. I chose *The Gold Rush*, a Charlie Chaplin movie that Dad introduced me to when I was nine. I have now seen *The Gold Rush* four times. I picked it the second and third times because I like the part when Charlie makes two dinner rolls dance across the table like a ballerina's legs.

This time I picked the movie because of Big

Jim. He and Charlie are best friends. They go prospecting for gold in the Yukon and run out of food. Big Jim is so hungry, he imagines Charlie is a giant chicken. He chases Charlie around their cabin trying to eat him. Luckily, Big Jim returns to normal just in time. After that, he and Charlie discover a mountain of gold under the snow. They share the money and remain best friends forever.

The first three times I saw *The Gold Rush*, the movie made me laugh. This time it made my eyes burn, because I don't have a best friend like Big Jim. I lost my best friend sticking up for a kid who punched me in the nose and won't even talk to me. I know Buddy has a good excuse for acting the way he does, and I would probably act the same way if I were him. But that doesn't make me feel any better about losing Alex.

After the movie, I went to my room, even though it was a half hour before my normal bedtime. While I was lying there in the dark, wishing I had rented a different video, Martha knocked on my door.

"What?" I called from bed.

"I want to talk about Ken."

"Ken who?"

"You know, Barbie's boyfriend."

"Oh, right. Ken."

"Can I come in?"

"Can't you tell me from there?"

"Okay. I was thinking that if Alex wants to go trick-or-treating with us, he could dress up as Ken's friend. I don't think Ken has any friends besides Barbie, but most grown-ups won't know that, so we'll be okay."

Good old Martha. I got out of bed and opened my door. Martha stood in the hallway, wearing her pink pajamas, staring up at me with her big brown eyes and a little smile on her face that said "pretty please." There was only one thing I could do.

"Forget Alex," I told her. "But I think it would be cool to go as Ken."

"Really?"

"Really."

"Yes!" She gave me a hug.

"Martha," Mom called. "Bedtime!"

Martha ran down the hall yelling, "Mom, guess what?"

Depressed as I was, all of a sudden I felt better.

11

this morning the Bar and Bat Mitzvah class studied the story of Abraham and Isaac. We read the passage where God commands Abraham to slaughter his son Isaac like a goat and offer him as a sacrifice on a stone altar. People took sides for and against God.

Josh Klickstein's side argued that it was right for God to test Abraham in that way, to make him prove that he deserved God's love. My side, which was led by Naomi Shrager, argued that it was wrong to order Abraham to do such a terrible thing to his son, even if God never meant to let him go all the way through with it. Abraham didn't deserve to be toyed with like that.

Mr. Nadler mostly agreed with Josh's side. He said great faith often requires great sacrifice. For instance, American soldiers sacrificed their lives fighting the Nazis in World War II to save democracy. That made sense to me, but I still thought God was cruel to make a good man like Abraham suffer.

The discussion about Abraham and Isaac made me think about Laura and Buddy. Did God let Laura die to test Buddy and his father? What would God do if they passed? What if they failed? Did God bring Buddy to Ms. Bobson's class to test me? I thought about asking the other kids these things, but I didn't because the questions were too hard. And I was too shy.

After class, Naomi Shrager came up to me.

"I'm having a Halloween party tomorrow night," she said. "You're invited."

"Thanks, but I have to take my sister trick-or-treating," I said.

"How sweet. Why don't you bring her along?"

Naomi told me the time and address of the party, which I forgot as soon as she said it.

•   •   •

Tonight Martha made me put on my good blue sweater, my best black pants, and my black lace-up shoes. She made me blow-dry my hair, too, and started calling me Ken as soon as we left the house. I felt dumb, but I tried my best to play along.

"Isn't it a beautiful night, Ken?" she asked.

"Yes, Barbie. It sure is."

"You look very handsome in your blue sweater."

"Thanks. You look great in that miniskirt."

"Thank you, Ken. I hoped you would like it."

I admit it was sort of fun going around with Martha. She was right about the candy. A lot of people thought we were so cute they gave us extra stuff. If only we hadn't stopped at 975 Garfield Street. The first time I had ever heard of Garfield Street I thought it was on the other side of town, not five blocks from my house.

A girl with two long braids, a fluffy blue dress, and red, sparkly shoes answered the door.

"Hi, Sam," she said, showing off her perfect teeth. "I'm so happy you could come."

"Hi, Naomi," I said, trying not to blush. "I didn't recognize you."

"I'm Dorothy."

"From *The Wizard of Oz*, of course," Martha chimed in.

"This is my sister, Martha," I explained.

"I thought so." Naomi's braids wiggled as she nodded. "Who are you two supposed to be?"

Martha rolled her eyes. "Can't you tell?"

"President and Hillary Clinton?"

"No, silly."

"Marilyn Monroe and Clark Gable?"

"Who?"

"They were old-time movie stars."

Martha took my hand. "We're Barbie and Ken."

"Oh, that's so sweet," said Naomi, beaming at Martha. "Come join the party."

"Thanks," chirped Martha, waltzing right in. "This is the first time I ever went trick-or-treating without my mom or my dad."

"Really?" said Naomi. "You seem so grown up."

That made Martha's night. Two minutes later

mine was ruined when I bumped into a pudgy vampire in the kitchen.

"Hey, Keeperman, what are you doing here?"

"Same thing you are, Warthog."

It turns out Andy is Naomi's next-door neighbor, so she invited him and his green-faced friend with the axe stuck in his head to her party.

"Hello, Mr. Green," said Martha.

"Hi, Martha."

"The name is Barbie, Alex."

"Sorry. How's it going, Barbie?"

"Ken and I got a lot of candy tonight."

"That's nice."

"You should have come with us."

"Ghouls don't belong with Ken and Barbie."

"You could have come as Ken's friend."

"I didn't know Ken had any friends."

"He does. His name is Ronnie."

The ghoul smirked at me with his yellow teeth and turned away. I drank a cup of pink lemonade to be polite, then told Martha it was time to leave.

"We have a nine o'clock curfew," she said to Naomi in a grown-up voice.

Naomi touched my arm. "It was wonderful to have you, Sam."

It's bad enough that Alex and I are enemies. Now Naomi thinks I really meant to show up at her party. Brother!

buddy was absent yesterday and today. I didn't miss him, but after school today the Farmdale Flyers sure did. We played the Hawthorne Eagles, one of the worst teams in the league. Without our best player, we lost 4-2.

Alex scored both of our goals. After the game, he started talking with me like we were friends again.

"You want to come over to my house?" he asked.

"I have to do my math," I told him.

"We can do it together."

"My parents think I should do my homework by myself."

"Since when?"

"It's a new policy."

It was a lie, and Alex knew it. My parents are happy when he and I do math homework together. That way they don't have to keep reminding me about it. But I didn't want to do my math with him. After having a fight, giving each other the silent treatment, and not going trick-or-treating together for the first time since we were in preschool, how could we suddenly be friends again without shaking hands and talking about what went wrong?

I know, I know. If I thought it was so important, then I should have been the one to say something. All I had to do was tell him that Buddy's mother was dead, and it would have probably changed everything. Alex would have understood. But I was still too angry at him to have a serious conversation.

Alex just wanted to pick up where we had left off. I wished I could have felt like that. I really wanted to forget what had happened and be best friends again. But I could still hear him bugging Buddy about the bird poop shirt even after I asked him to stop. And I could still see him goofing around with Warthog and Lizard on the playground instead of playing with me. So I went home and did my math homework by myself, and that was that.

Buddy didn't show up for school today, again. Ms. Bobson wrote his address on the front board.

"I'll bet he would appreciate some get-well cards," she said.

Alex raised his hand before she had even finished her sentence. "Do we have to?"

"No, Alex, it's only a suggestion. But I hope you will. In case you haven't noticed, Buddy has been having trouble in school."

I thought Ms. Bobson was going to say something about Laura. That's what I was hoping, at least. I was tired of keeping the secret to myself. I wanted other people to know what had happened to her, to see Buddy the way I see him. I wanted them to get the same kind of stomach cramps that I get when I think about what it would be like to go to bed knowing I won't see my mom in the morning.

But Ms. Bobson didn't say anything else. She

just stood by the board, waiting. And I couldn't tell if she didn't know that Laura was dead, or if she didn't want to tell the class for some of the same reasons I haven't.

Jane Herbert, the teacher's pet, was the first one to write down the address. Her friend Rita Lopez was next. Most of the other girls wrote it down, too. Besides Jason Rush, there was only one other boy who did it, the one who kept hearing Laura White's voice inside his head telling him, "You're a nice boy, Sammy, a nice boy."

13

a t synagogue this morning the Bar and Bat Mitzvah class talked about the death of Abraham's wife, Sarah. After she died, Abraham bought a cave called Machpelah to bury her in. Machpelah is in the town of Hebron, which used to be part of Israel. Mr. Nadler said the Israelis gave almost all of Hebron to the Palestinians a few years ago to make peace.

The class split into sides to debate whether it was a good or bad idea to give away most of Hebron. Josh Klickstein's side argued that Israel should have kept all of it because Hebron is a holy city to the Jews, and Israel is a Jewish country. Naomi Shrager's side argued that the Palestinians deserved all of Hebron because they are related to Abraham's son Ishmael and have a right to the land, too.

I had a hard time choosing sides. In the end, I sat with Josh's group to stay away from Naomi. I didn't say much. The whole time the class was debating I couldn't get Sarah and her son Isaac out of my mind. Mr. Nadler told us that after Sarah died, her family's tent became a cold, dark place. He said that a holy cloud that once glowed around her door like a heavenly welcome sign vanished. Guests were no longer welcome, and Isaac was very sad. Sarah and Isaac stayed in my mind for the rest of the day.

Last night I dreamed that Isaac was sitting on the ground in his tent. He wouldn't eat or talk. He just sat there staring into space. Suddenly, he looked up, motioned in my direction, and kicked a soccer ball to me. My eyes popped open.

I fell back to sleep after that, but I didn't forget the dream. This morning I remembered every detail right down to the way Isaac sat in his tent with his shoulders hunched over.

The dream got me thinking about Buddy. I wondered what he dreamed about and whether his dreams were happy or sad, or if he forgot them the minute he woke up in the morning.

Before breakfast I started making a card. I'm not a very good artist. It took me three tries before I got the soccer player standing in the middle of a field the way I wanted him. I also had a hard time deciding what to put in the player's dialogue balloon. Finally, I wrote: *Feel Better, Buddy.*

I could have dropped the envelope in the mailbox down at the corner, but since it's Sunday and there's no mail pickup, I decided to bike over and deliver it by hand to make sure Buddy got it sooner than later.

The address Ms. Bobson gave us was Mr. White's shoe shop. There was a CLOSED sign in the window, but Mr. White was shining shoes at his spinning brush machine. I had to keep pounding on the door with my fist before he finally heard me. As soon as he noticed me, he nodded toward the CLOSED sign and kept on working.

I had to knock even harder to get his attention again. When he saw me still standing there, he shook his finger at the sign. I showed him I had something to deliver. Finally, he shut off his machine and opened the door.

"What is it?" he asked. His voice sounded baked and dry, like the desert.

"This is for Buddy," I said, giving him the envelope.

He studied it carefully. "Who are you?"

"Sam Keeperman. I'm in Buddy's class." Mr. White looked at me kind of funny.

"We're on the same soccer team, too," I told him.

His lips wrinkled, but I couldn't tell if he was grinning or trying not to cry.

"Do you want to deliver it yourself, Sam?" He pointed to a stairway at the back of the shop. "Buddy's upstairs."

Mr. White is the exact opposite of Laura. He has a sharp, bony face that looks like it might crack if he ever really smiles. Words stumbled from his mouth like they didn't want to come out. He made me feel weird. There was no way I was going up those back stairs.

"I have to get home," I said.

Mr. White called out something as I rode down the street, but I didn't hear what he said. I was too far away.

14

buddy missed class again yesterday, but he came back today. He didn't say thanks for the card, or smile, or anything, but at soccer practice he gave me so many perfect passes that I scored six goals during our scrimmage.

Mr. Taylor said "Terrific!" so many times that Alex started mimicking him. Then Warthog joined in. Whenever Mr. Taylor turned his back, they snuck up to me and whispered, "Terrific!"

"Stop it," I said.

"Terrific," whispered Alex.

"Terrific," oinked Warthog.

"Shut up, snoutnose."

I didn't care about Andy. He isn't my friend

to begin with. But I was so mad at Alex that if Mr. Taylor wasn't there, I probably would have punched him. Jealous jerk.

After practice, when Mr. White came to pick up Buddy, instead of driving off right away, he got out of his car and called my name. I was so angry at Alex by then that I didn't want to talk to anyone. I jumped on my bike and rode home.

Today at school things got worse. Everywhere I went—in the hallway, our classroom, the cafeteria, the playground, the bathroom—Alex was there whispering, "Mr. Terrific! Mr. Terrific!! Mr. Terrific!!!"

He did it so much, other kids started calling me Mr. Terrific.

"Alex," I said. "Why are you doing this?"

"Doing what?" he asked, like Mr. Innocent.

"I thought we were best friends."

"That's right, Mr. Terrific. We were."

After all that had happened between me and Alex, there was no way I could go to our soccer game after school today with him there. So I came straight home. I phoned Mr. Taylor and left a message on his answering machine that I had a bad stomachache. Then I went upstairs to my room and listened to the Beatles' *Sergeant Pepper's Lonely Hearts Club Band.*

Dad gave me the CD when I was eight. He said that whenever he listened to the Beatles, they made him smile. I was in the middle of playing the CD for the fourth time, and still not smiling, when my door opened and Mom poked her head into the room. She waited until I turned down the volume.

"You've got a visitor." Her voice was very quiet.

"Who is it?"

"Mr. White."

"I've got a stomachache."

"The man wants to talk to you."

"I can't get up."

"Sam."

"I'm serious."

"If you're in such pain, then I think we should go to the doctor's. It could be appendicitis."

"What?"

"Hurry up, he's waiting." She knew I was faking.

Mr. White stood in the middle of the living room as I limped down the stairs. Mom gave me a look. She knew the limp was an act, too.

"Sorry to hear you're sick," said Mr. White.

He threw back his shoulders like he was shaking off rain and handed me a folded sheet of lined yellow notepaper.

"Buddy asked me to give you this."

"Thanks."

I could tell Mom wanted me to unfold the note and read it right then, but I didn't want to. So we all stood around without saying anything until she finally broke the silence.

"It was so kind of you to stop by, Mr. White," Mom said. "You really didn't have to go to such trouble. You must have so many other things—"

"No trouble," interrupted Mr. White. Turning toward me he said, "Hope you feel better, Sam."

Then he walked to the door.

Mom opened it for him. "I just want to tell you again," she said, "how sorry we are about Laura."

He nodded. "Thank you, Mrs. Keeperman."

We watched him trudge down the sidewalk to his car. Buddy sat in the front seat. He looked at me and lifted his hand to wave as they pulled away.

Mom started asking questions as soon as they left.

"When did you and Buddy White become friends?"

"We're not friends, exactly."

"Why did he drop off that note?"

"Probably because I dropped one off at his house the other day."

"Why?"

"Because he missed school, and Ms. Bobson said we should make him get-well cards."

"What does his note say?"

"I don't know. I haven't had a chance to read it yet."

Mom took the hint and left to go pick up Martha at tap dance class.

The folded sheet had my name written in pencil on the front. Below my name were the words:

Laptham Raptors: 3
Farmdale Fliers: 1

Inside there were two soccer players standing on both ends of a bright green field. The blades of grass looked almost real. A dialogue balloon floating over one of the figures read: Feel Better, Sam. Buddy was a pretty good artist.

I left the note on the kitchen table for Mom to see and went back up to my room.

At bedtime Mom and Dad came in together to say good night, which is something they almost never do.

"We wanted you to know how proud we are of you," Mom said.

Dad ruffled my hair. "You're a good man, Sam."

"All I did was make him a card."

"The little things count," said Mom, kissing me.

Dad kissed me, too. "The little things can make all the difference."

We snuggled together in the bed for a while without talking, Dad on one side of me, Mom on the other. Cramped as we were, it felt good having them both there like that—warm, safe.

It didn't take too long before Dad started snoring. Mom shook him. "Bob."

"Huh? What?"

"Go sleep in your own bed."

"Right."

He sat up, mumbled, "See you in the morning, champ," and sleepwalked out of the room.

Mom giggled as Dad stumbled across the hall to their bedroom, then she was quiet again. As I listened to her breathing beside me, a hundred thoughts floated around in my head trying to get out. "Mom," I finally said. "I know about Laura."

"I know you do."

"You're not mad at Dad for telling me, are you?"

"No. It's better this way." Mom put her arm around my shoulder. "He was right to tell you."

"I've been thinking about her a lot lately," I said.

"So have I."

"Dad says he doesn't know if her soul is in heaven or not."

"Neither do I."

"Then where could it be?"

"In eternity."

"Where's that?"

"A place beyond space and time."

"Do you think she can see us from where she is?"

"Perhaps. But she may be too busy watching over Buddy."

I wasn't sure I believed her, but it was still a pretty good answer, good enough for right then.

After that, we snuggled tight, letting the night sounds surround us, before Mom hugged me once more and sat up. The mattress sighed as she got out of bed.

"Sweet dreams," she said, touching my cheek with hers.

I felt a little less rotten about the day as she walked out of the room, except the words "Mr. Terrific" kept echoing in my head until sleep stopped my thoughts.

i hoped my parents would let me skip synagogue this morning because I had been nice
to Buddy. Nope. Dad gave me a lecture about
how going to services is an important responsi-
bility, how it teaches good values and creates a
spirit of community blah blah blah. I got the
message: no.

The Bar and Bat Mitzvah class talked about
Isaac and Rebecca's twin sons, Jacob and Esau.
The two of them were so jealous of each other
that they started fighting in their mother's womb
to see who would come out first. Esau won, but
Jacob came out right behind him, holding on to
his brother's heel.

From that day on the two boys were always

competing. To make things worse, their parents picked favorites. Isaac loved Esau because he was a good hunter, and Rebecca favored Jacob because he was gentle.

When Isaac was about to die, he called Esau to give him a final blessing before God. The final blessing was like an inheritance. Rebecca wanted Jacob to get it, because she knew it would bring him good fortune. So she dressed him in Esau's clothes and sent him to Isaac who was too blind to tell that it was Jacob in disguise when he blessed him.

After he stole his brother's inheritance, Jacob had to run away so Esau wouldn't kill him. Esau had a terrible temper.

There was no debate. Everyone in class agreed that Esau and Jacob's parents were wrong to choose favorites. Jealousy can destroy a family. It can also destroy a friendship. I know.

Today our family drove to Governor Dodge Park to see the autumn colors. We were all excited when we left the house after breakfast. Too bad most of the trees were already bare.

That seems to happen to us every year. We always get the idea to go see the leaves a week too late. It never really bothered me before. But this year the trees' skeleton branches and the dead leaves on the ground made me sad.

I guess it was because I've had Laura on my mind so much. All I needed to do was take a walk in the woods to start thinking about her again.

When I started thinking about her, I realized that in the end I didn't know Laura very well. I mean, we used to talk a lot, but most of the time I was usually answering one of her questions. I hardly ever asked her about herself. It was kind of the same way with the leaves. I didn't really see them until after they had fallen off their branches.

Some of the oak trees still had leaves—bright red ones the color of the sun right before it sets. Martha and I each collected a handful off the ground to save for making collages. When she fell asleep in the car on the way home, the leaves dropped out of her hand and landed in a clump on the floor. They made me think of Laura again.

16

It started to drizzle on my way to school this morning. By the time I got there, it was pouring, and my sneakers were soaked.

At recess it rained so hard we had to play inside. The gym is okay for phys ed class, but it's lousy for recess, really loud and crowded. Things were not going well.

After lunch, Ms. Bobson introduced our new science project: crystal growing. She assigned project partners. I got Buddy. No question about it. This was not turning out to be my lucky day.

I boiled our sugar-water solutions, poured them into a jar with orange food coloring, and added two pieces of string for the crystals to grow on. Buddy said nothing the whole time. But when it was time to make a grid to record our crystals' progress, he took a ruler out of his desk and drew a straight line down the left side of our graph paper.

I was too surprised to say anything, so I just watched him draw five more vertical lines and sixteen horizontal lines across the page to make boxes for all the days left in the month. He did a nice, careful job.

Ms. Bobson walked over with a big smile.

"That's an excellent chart, boys," she said.

Buddy and I both shrugged.

While he was writing the names of the days at the top of each column, I looked up. All the other kids were staring at us.

Buddy didn't seem to care, but I felt so embarrassed I wanted to run out of the room. Instead, I sat up very straight and stared right back even when Alex mouthed the words, "Mr. Terrific."

Thank God the bell rang after that. People stopped staring as we all put away our materials. But I still felt weird, especially after Buddy followed me out of class and handed me a note. I waited until he and everybody else had disappeared down the hall before I opened it. It said,

I have a quartz collection. You want to come over to my house and see it?

I was so stunned that I avoided Buddy for the rest of the day.

Tonight at dinner I told my parents that Buddy invited me to his house to see his quartz collection.

"Cool," said Dad.

"Is he the boy who doesn't talk?" asked Martha.

"Yes."

"When did he start talking?"

"He hasn't yet."

"Then how did he invite you to come over?"

"He wrote me a note."

"Why doesn't he talk?"

I looked at Dad. He looked at Mom. She nodded at me like it was okay to tell.

"I think it's because he's sad."

"Why is he sad?"

"Because he lost his mom."

"Where did he lose her?"

"She got killed in a car accident."

"Like Laura did?"

"Yes, love," said Dad. "Buddy is Laura's son."

"Oh."

Martha took a bite of her baked potato and chewed it slowly. Mom and Dad watched her like they were trying to read her mind. Finally, she swallowed and asked, "What's a quartz collection?"

That Martha. I never know what she's going to say next.

dark clouds stared down at me when I left the house this morning, but I got to school before the thunderstorm hit. Ms. Bobson brought in chocolate donuts and apple cider for a treat.

"I thought this might help cheer up a gloomy fall morning," she said. I think everyone knew the treats were also in honor of Buddy picking up a pencil for the first time yesterday.

In art class Buddy painted a picture of a soccer field covered with giant soccer balls. If it wasn't for the goalposts at each end of the field, I would have said it was a herd of cows in a pasture. Ms. Moberley made a big deal over it.

"Buddy, your colors are wonderful," she said.

She must have patted him on the back ten times. Buddy didn't say anything, but I saw him smile a little. It was his first project in art class.

The rain finally stopped by the end of school, but everything smelled damp. The ground was too soggy for soccer practice. Buddy was standing on the sidewalk in his hunched over way when I came out of the building.

I reached into my pocket for my keys. As I unlocked my bike, I felt a tap on the shoulder.

"Well?"

Buddy's voice was deeper than I expected, and it sounded baked and dry, just like his dad's. When I turned to look at him, he had a funny expression on his face. I couldn't tell if he was trying to smile or struggling not to. Either way, his lips were crooked. His eyes reminded me of Martha's when she's asking for a special favor.

"Okay," I said. "Let's go."

Buddy didn't have a bike, so I walked mine back to his house to see his quartz collection. Buddy kept looking at my bike out of the corner of his eye. It's a pretty cool saffron yellow mountain bike with left- and right-handed grip shifts that make gear changes really smooth. "You want to take a ride?" I asked.

He smiled and climbed on. The bike was two sizes too big for him, but he did okay, except when he got to the corner of Broom Street. Buddy was trying so hard to keep his balance that he didn't see the traffic light change.

"Watch out!" I cried.

The bike skidded to a stop with the help of a city mailbox. Buddy got up from the accident without a scratch, but my bike frame wound up with a blue streak that was not part of the paint job.

"Sorry," he said.

"Don't worry about it." I shrugged. "The blue looks good, like a lightning bolt."

Buddy thought about it for a while, then nodded.

Mr. White was sewing new soles on a pair of penny loafers when we walked into his shop. His hands were black with polish. A mound of shoes lay on a long table beside him.

"Hello, Sam," he said, looking up. He wiped

his right hand across his apron and offered it to me. "Welcome."

"Thanks," I said as we shook.

"There's a snack upstairs," he said, then went back to what he was doing.

With only Buddy and his dad around to take care of it, I expected the upstairs apartment to be sloppy, but it was the exact opposite. The living room carpet looked like it had just been vacuumed. The windows were spotless, and the magazines on the coffee table were stacked perfectly. The walls were bright yellow, a cheerful color that reminded me of Laura's hellos.

Two caramel apples waited on a square piece of wax paper in the kitchen. We sat at the table to eat them. My apple was humongous, and the caramel was so thick, it took me four bites to eat through it. I made a fish face when I bit into the tart fruit. Buddy smiled and did the same thing.

In Jewish homes we attach *mezuzahs* to our doorposts as a sign of our love for God. I thought the Whites would have crosses hanging on every wall, but I didn't see any. I wanted to ask Buddy why. I also wanted to ask him what it feels like to never celebrate holidays or birthdays, but I didn't think it would be a good idea.

As soon as we finished eating the caramel apples, Buddy threw the sticks and wax paper away.

"You ready to see my collection now?" he asked.

"Sure."

"Come on."

Buddy led me to his room, which was as neat as the rest of the house. His quartz collection had everything from rock crystal and milky quartz to agate, opal, and jasper, and I can't remember what else. There were more than a hundred different rocks and minerals. All of them were carefully mounted on shelves in egg cartons and shoe boxes that were open like books so I could see inside. Every specimen had a piece of white tape with a number written on it. The numbers matched file cards that had information about each specimen, like its color, its luster, its hardness, where Buddy found it, and when. Some of the handwriting looked like a kid's, and some of it looked like an adult's.

"This is great," I said. "Just like the geology museum downtown."

"My mom helped."

Buddy picked up a purple amethyst and held it in front of a lamp. Little specks of light glittered all over it like fireflies.

"This was her favorite," he said.

"I knew your mom."

"I know."

Buddy put the amethyst back in its carton. I thought I'd said something wrong. While Buddy straightened all the boxes on his shelves, even the ones that were already perfect, I pretended to study a piece of rose-colored onyx shaped like a half-moon. Suddenly, Buddy stopped what he was doing and looked at me.

"After the accident, I thought she wasn't dead," he said. "I told myself she was in Minnesota on vacation."

"Where do you think she is now?"

"With God."

"Up in heaven?"

"I don't believe in heaven."

"Then where could she be?"

"In God's memory."

"Where's that?"

He shrugged.

I tried to imagine God's memory. The best picture I could come up with was the biggest computer in the universe, but I knew that was wrong. It was like trying to imagine eternity. How can you describe a place beyond space and time?

Mr. White came upstairs. He puttered around the kitchen before he called to us. We found him by the sink slicing onions.

"I'm making tuna casserole for dinner," he said. "You want to join us, Sam?"

"I have to bike home before dark," I said.

"I can drive you."

"Thanks, but my mom's expecting me."

I liked seeing Buddy's rock and mineral collection, and I didn't want to hurt his feelings, but I didn't feel like eating dinner with him and his dad. The three of us were still mostly strangers. I was relieved when Mr. White dropped the subject. A few minutes later Buddy walked me downstairs.

"Thanks for the tour," I said as I unlocked my bike.

He studied the blue streak of paint on my bike frame. "Sorry about that," he said.

"Don't worry about it," I told him.

He sighed. "You were smart not to stay."

"Why?"

"Because we'd only make you sad."

Then he shrugged and went back upstairs without saying good-bye.

18

this morning Motor Mouth Martha was so excited about the Thanksgiving play her class is rehearsing for next week that she couldn't eat breakfast. The first-graders' play is about how the Pilgrims came to America and built the town of Plymouth. Martha is going to play Miles Standish, the man who taught the settlers how to hunt and survive in the wilderness. She was worried that the shoulders on her costume didn't look big enough.

"You're supposed to be a Pilgrim," I said, "not a Green Bay Packer."

"Miles Standish was a very strong leader. He should look like a Green Bay Packer," she told me.

"There were no Green Bay Packers back then."

"I don't care. I like the Green Bay Packers."

So Mom sewed padding inside the shoulders of her costume while I helped Martha practice her lines. She spoke in this funny deep voice, but I wasn't allowed to laugh, because the play is not a comedy. My favorite line is, "Hey, why don't we all chill out and have a big party?" They're doing a modern version of the Thanksgiving story.

Anyway, my day started out pretty good thanks to Martha, but things changed as soon as I got to school. For social studies, we've been reading a time traveler book about the Spanish Inquisition. At the end of each chapter you have choices about which page to turn to next. When Ms. Bobson asked for a volunteer to read, Buddy raised his hand. I thought Ms. Bobson's head might fall off, she nodded at him so many times. Everybody was watching Buddy.

"You're standing in the town square of Seville," he began slowly. "The year is 1481. Evening approaches and a light snow is falling."

Buddy is not the best reader in class, but he's still pretty good. There was no reason to make fun of him. After he finished, a few of the kids gave him a thumbs-up. Not Alex. On the way to lunch, he made faces behind Buddy's back and mimicked the way he read. I tried to ignore him, but it was really hard. All day long, every time I turned around, there was Alex, making faces. I couldn't keep Laura to myself any longer.

"Alex," I said.

"Yes, Mr. Terrific?"

"I have to tell you a secret about Buddy."

Alex held up his hand like a traffic cop. "The secret is that you love him."

"What?"

"You love him."

"I do not!"

Alex smiled like a goofball and stumbled off holding his hands over his heart. He made me so mad and sad that I felt like fighting and crying at the same time.

After school, I thought about skipping soccer to stay out of trouble, but then I said to myself, No way! Why should I let Alex keep me from doing something I like? He doesn't own the world.

We started practice with one of my favorite drills. Two players pass the ball back and forth while they run down the field, and two defenders try to stop them before they can score a goal. Buddy and I were passing partners, and Lizard was in the goal. Warthog ran up to cover Buddy. Alex took me.

"Okay, Mr. Terrific," he said. "Show me your stuff."

"Just watch," I told him.

Buddy and I passed the ball back and forth three times and made it up to midfield. He was on the right wing and I was in the center as we set up for a give-and-go. Buddy kicked the ball to me and dashed for the goal, but I never had a chance to return the pass, because Alex knocked me down. It was no accident. He ran over me like I was a weed. I hit the ground so hard, I lost my breath.

I can't remember everything that happened after that, but I do know that as soon as I got up something snapped in me. I charged Alex and smashed my head into his stomach. Then Buddy jumped in, and the three of us fell on the ground punching and kicking.

When Mr. Taylor finally separated us, Alex had a bloody ear and a huge lump on his forehead.

"I don't care who started it," said Mr. Taylor. "All three of you are off the team."

Alex tried to argue, but when he talked it sounded like he was drunk.

Mr. Taylor took Alex to the hospital for an X ray. As soon as they left, I turned on Buddy.

"Who told you to butt into my fight?" I yelled.

"I was trying to help," he said quietly.

"Some help! If it wasn't for you, I would never have gotten into that fight in the first place!"

I don't remember what else I said exactly, but I know Buddy was crying by the time I rode off on my bike, and so was I. At home I blubbered so hard that it took a half hour just to explain that Mr. Taylor had kicked me off the team.

"Why?" asked Mom.

"I got into a fight with Alex," I sobbed.

"Over what?"

"I don't want to talk about it."

"Do you want me to call Mr. Taylor and see what I can do?" asked Dad.

"No. I'm off the team, and that's that."

"You sure?"

"Yes. Mr. Taylor means what he says."

Martha got so upset when she saw me crying that she started crying, too.

"Please, Sam," she begged. "Let Daddy call him."

"No!"

I made Dad promise not to call, then I ran to my room, locked the door, and cranked the Beatles up to full volume.

19

I didn't want to go to school today, but Mom and Dad said I had to unless I was sick.

"If I go, Alex will make me sick," I told them.

"No, he won't," Mom said.

"Yes, he will."

"How can you say that about Alex?"

"Because he's sickening."

"So what happened?" asked Dad.

"I don't want to talk about it."

"Do you want to talk about it with me?" asked Martha.

"No."

I didn't talk to anybody the whole day at school, either. But at least I didn't have to see Alex or Buddy. They were both absent.

• • •

This morning I still felt so bad I wouldn't get out of bed. Mom and Dad let me skip synagogue, but that didn't help me feel any better. I spent the whole day in my room, and everyone, Martha included, left me alone.

Today I sat in the den like a stone watching TV and stuffing my mouth with junk food. I didn't want to eat dinner, but Mom still made me sit at the table with everyone. I asked my parents if I could transfer to another school. They said no, of course.

"Why not?" I asked.

"Because Farmdale is a good school," said Dad.

"No, it isn't."

"What's wrong with Farmdale?" asked Martha.

"It stinks."

"It does not."

"Yes, it does. Alex Kohler spoiled it."

"How?"

"By being a jerk."

"Does that mean you're not best friends anymore?"

"Martha, eat your mashed potatoes," I said.

Leave it to her to ask the toughest question.

Alex came back to class today. He wore a bandage on his ear and had a black-and-blue mark across his forehead shaped like an exclamation point.

"What happened to you?" asked Ms. Bobson.

"I had a concussion," he said. "And they gave me three stitches in my ear."

"My goodness. Were you in an accident?"

"No, I got into a fight at soccer practice."

"Over what?"

"Something stupid."

People laughed.

"Stop that!" ordered Ms. Bobson.

The class got quiet. Alex looked down at his desk. Ms. Bobson dropped the subject, but I could tell she felt sorry for him.

I didn't know how I should feel. One part of me thought Alex got what he deserved. The other part was sorry to hear he had a concussion and stitches. I never wanted us to be enemies. During recess we passed each other twice on the playground, but neither of us said anything.

After school, while I biked home by myself, I heard someone behind me sneeze. I knew who it was.

"What do you want, Alex?" I asked, without turning around.

"Nothing," he said.

"Then stop following me."

"I'm not following you."

I crossed the street and pedaled faster. Alex pedaled faster, too. Pretty soon we were riding at the same pace on opposite sides of the road. Then we were racing. The houses passed in a blur. Crossing Adams Street, I didn't even bother to look for cars. I just kept pedaling. Alex gave up at the next block, and I rode the rest of the way home alone.

20

today, when Buddy didn't show up at school again, I had to do something. I knew one reason he was absent had to do with me. Like he said, he was only trying to help. After the last bell, I went up to Ms. Bobson and offered to take Buddy's homework assignments to him.

"That's very nice of you, Sam," she said, "but Buddy's father has already seen to that."

I rode over to his house after school, anyway. Mr. White looked up from his shoes and nodded at me as I walked in.

"What can I do for you, Sam?"

"Is Buddy home?"

"Upstairs."

"Can I see him?"

"Fine with me, but I can't speak for Buddy."

The kitchen was empty.

"Hello," I called.

A door slammed.

"Buddy?"

No answer.

"Buddy?" I called more loudly.

"What?" His voice came from the bathroom.

"I came to say hi."

No answer.

"And to tell you I'm sorry."

He still wouldn't answer.

"Buddy?"

I sat on the floor outside the bathroom. I heard him clear his throat.

"Okay," he said.

"You want to come out?"

"No."

"All right."

I waited.

"Guess what?" I said. "Our sugar crystals grew two centimeters."

I waited some more, but Buddy didn't say anything else, so I gave up and walked back downstairs. Mr. White didn't stop working as I passed by his table. Why did I bother? I thought as I left the shop. Why did I even bother?

"That was fast," a voice called as I was unlocking my bike.

I looked back and saw Buddy standing in the doorway of the shoe shop.

"What was fast?" I asked.

"Our crystals."

"It was, wasn't it?" I said.

"What happened to Alex?"

"He got a concussion and three stitches."

Buddy's eyes grew big. "We make a pretty good team, don't we?" he said.

"Yeah." I smiled. "I guess we do."

"See you tomorrow."

"Tomorrow."

As I got on my bike Buddy eyed my bike frame.

"Nice lightning bolt," he said.

Tonight the Farmdale Elementary School first-graders put on their Thanksgiving play. Martha was a great Miles Standish, except she had a hard time keeping her beard on. I thought that made the play better, except, well, it wasn't supposed to be a comedy.

Afterward we went out for pumpkin pie and ice cream at Eureka Joe's. Miss Motor Mouth told our waitress, Jeanie, all about the Pilgrims and about her part. She even recited some of her lines. Jeanie asked for an autograph. Martha had me write a personal message on a napkin:

To Jeanie,
You have great desserts.
Best regards, Miles Standish

Martha signed her own name, too.

While we ate our pie and ice cream, Naomi Shrager walked in with that guy Roscoe Something-or-Other who used to play on the Wildcats' soccer team. Naomi spotted me and dragged Roscoe along with her to our booth.

"Hi, Sam," she said.

"Hi."

"Is that you, Barbie?"

"Please call me Miles Standish now," said Martha.

"All right. Mr. Standish, this is my boyfriend, Roscoe."

"Hello, Roscoe." Martha shook his hand. "I like your name."

"Thanks, Miles," said Roscoe. "I like yours, too."

Naomi introduced herself to my parents and flashed them one of her smiles. "Mr. and Mrs. Keeperman, you've got the two sweetest kids."

"Thanks," said Dad.

"We know," said Mom.

"Any time you need a baby-sitter, I'm available."

Martha's eyes looked like sparklers. "Yes!"

"We'll keep it in mind," said Mom.

"Nice meeting you," said Dad.

Naomi and Roscoe headed for an empty booth in back. I couldn't figure out if I felt relieved or annoyed. All along I thought Naomi had a crush on me, and now she was talking about baby-sitting for Martha *and* me. Or did I hear her wrong? Anyway, after thinking about it for a while, I decided to consider it a good omen.

21

this morning I asked Mom if we could fit a few more people at our Thanksgiving table. She said sure, so I called the Whites and invited them. Buddy said that he and his dad were busy. I had a feeling they wouldn't come, but that's okay. At least I made the offer.

Even without the Whites, our dining room was packed tonight. Grandpa Jules and Grandma Pauline drove up from Chicago with Uncle Ernie, Aunt Louise, and all of the cousins. Our neighbors the Nelsons came over, too.

Martha entertained everyone at dinner by putting on her costume and reciting her lines from the Thanksgiving play. When her beard fell into the cranberry sauce I tried not to laugh, but I couldn't help myself. And I wasn't the only one. Good old Motor Mouth didn't mind. She just kept on going.

During dessert the phone rang. It was Buddy.

"Sorry I couldn't make it tonight," he said.

"That's okay," I told him.

"We're Jehovah's Witnesses."

"I know."

"We don't celebrate Thanksgiving."

"Because you think it's pagan?"

"How did you know?"

"It was something your mom said."

"Oh."

He was quiet for a minute. Then he said, "You want to play soccer tomorrow in the park?"

"What time?"

"How about ten o'clock?"

"Sure."

This morning was sunny and really warm for the last week of November. Buddy showed up at the park wearing my old bird poop T-shirt over a long-sleeve jersey. I tried not to stare, but I couldn't help peeking at it as we trotted around the field flicking short passes back and forth.

"My mom told me she got this shirt at a yard sale," Buddy said after a while, like he'd been reading my thoughts.

"Seriously?"

"Seriously."

"Brother."

My stomach got tight thinking how he must have felt at soccer practice the day Alex made a big deal about that shirt. I clumsily kicked a squibbler out-of-bounds, and we both raced after it. Buddy beat me, but not by much. Once we were back in our passing rhythm, he started talking again.

"I was so embarrassed that day at practice, I felt like I was going to throw up," he said.

"I don't blame you."

"My mom didn't tell me where she got the shirt because she was ashamed to accept charity."

"It wasn't really charity," I said.

"What was it, then?"

"More like recycling."

Buddy gave me a look. "Well, whatever you call it, she didn't tell me the truth."

We passed the ball around for a while without talking. A blackbird landed in a tree next to the field and started to sing. I don't usually pay attention to blackbirds, but that one caught my ear, and I slowed down to listen. Buddy slowed down, too.

"What is it?" he asked.

I pointed to the bird. "It sounds sad."

We listened some more.

"It sounds angry," Buddy said.

"You think so?"

"Yeah."

Buddy booted the ball upfield into the goal. The bird flew to another tree and kept on singing.

"Sometimes at night I yell like that," Buddy said.

"Why?"

"I'm angry. At my mom."

"Just because she didn't tell you about my T-shirt?"

"No, because she killed herself."

"Who said she killed herself?"

"If she ran over that deer instead of driving around it, she never would have hit a tree."

"That's not the same thing as killing herself."

"Yeah, I know. And recycling isn't charity."

He ran after the soccer ball. By the time I caught up to him he was sitting on the grass bouncing the ball off of one of the goalposts.

"Sorry," I said.

"You didn't do anything."

"I'm still sorry."

He tossed me the ball. I bounced it off of the goalpost a few times, then tossed it back to him.

"You want to know something?" he said.

"What?"

"The day I found out the truth about your T-shirt, I threw it in the garbage."

"I probably would have done the same thing."

"But I took it out because I really like it."

"Me, too," I said.

"The blue jay poop is my favorite."

"I like the warbler's."

We both smiled about that, then practiced our long kicks. Launching the ball back and forth across the field, we didn't talk, but I kept thinking about what Buddy had said about Laura and the T-shirt. It made me feel so weird, I wished he had worn something else.

When we took a break, I asked him why he switched to Farmdale School.

"My dad thought I needed a fresh start," he said.

"Are you happy you did it?"

He shrugged in a way that kind of looked like a nod. "My dad also thought playing for the Flyers would be good for me."

"Was it?"

"Maybe. But I might not play on the team next year."

"Seriously?"

"Seriously."

"Why not?"

"Because organized sports isn't something people like me usually do."

"How come?"

"Witnesses think competition weakens the spirit."

"What does that mean?"

"It means that playing on a team can make

you so stuck-up that you forget about God." Buddy stopped talking to retie one of his shoelaces, then quietly added, "At least, that's what my mom always said."

"Then why did your dad want you to play on the team?"

"He said I needed something to keep me from thinking so much and that God would understand."

Buddy stared at me like he was waiting to hear my opinion. Actually, I thought that dropping off the team would be a mistake, not to mention bad news for the Farmdale Flyers. Besides, not everybody who plays organized sports has to be stuck-up. But I was afraid if I told Buddy that, it would sound like I was taking sides against his mom. So I didn't say anything and just gave one of those shrugs that kind of looked like a nod.

A little later Alex and Andy showed up. I was afraid they were going to say something about Buddy's shirt, but they challenged us to a game instead. It was a good, close game. Buddy and I won, 10-8.

When Mr. White came by, instead of taking Buddy right home, he hung around so we could keep playing. Buddy and I won three games out of five. By then the sun was so hot we were all sweating. We sprayed each other from the water fountain to cool off.

After Buddy and his dad drove off, Andy got picked up by his mom. That left you-know-who and me alone.

"You want to ride home together?" asked Alex.

I shrugged and climbed on my bike. We rode for a couple of blocks before he started talking.

"You were right, Sam," said Alex. "I acted like a jerk."

"Why did you?"

"Because I thought you liked Buddy more than me."

"His mom died."

Alex slowed down. "What?"

"She got killed in a car accident last summer."

"Why didn't you tell me that in the first place?"

"I guess I was a jerk, too."

When we got to my house, we sat on the

front steps. Alex showed me the stitches in his ear, which looked kind of cool. Then he told me how they x-rayed his head at the hospital, and I told him about Buddy's rock and mineral collection while the sun dried our soggy clothes.

In synagogue this morning the Bar and Bat Mitzvah class talked about how Jacob and Esau made up after not seeing each other for a long time. Jacob sent Esau hundreds of goats, sheep, cows, camels, and other animals as a peace offering. When they finally met, they hugged and kissed, but they were never really friends after that.

People in class tried to figure out why Jacob and Esau could never be close even though they were twins. Basically, we agreed that they didn't have much in common besides the same parents.

I think Alex and I have more in common than Jacob and Esau had, but that doesn't mean we'll become best friends again. I'm definitely not sending him any goats, or camels, or anything. Maybe I'll send a card.

And what about Buddy? Now that he and I have made up, I wonder if we can become real friends. We'll see.

Now that I've thought about it some more, I don't feel so weird about Buddy and my old T-shirt. Laura didn't tell him the truth about it because she had pride. It's as simple as that. If Buddy and I had been friends back then, I might have given him the shirt myself.

I don't understand why Laura had to die trying to save that deer, and I probably never will. But I do know that she's not in Minnesota planning to come home and surprise Buddy. Whether she's resting in a world beyond time and space, or she's locked in God's memory, or she's floating around in heaven depends on what you believe.

And maybe it's no great discovery, but something else came to me last Saturday about Laura and Buddy. It happened when Mom and Dad decided to stay home with me and Martha instead of hiring a baby-sitter and going out by themselves. We ordered pizza, rented a movie, and snuggled under a blanket together on the couch in the den while we watched the film.

I think everyone was trying to be extra nice to me after what I went through with Buddy. That's the only reasonable explanation I can come up with for why no one complained when I said I wanted to rent *Modern Times*.

I've now seen the movie seven times, but so what? A classic is a classic. My favorite part is when Charlie Chaplin lands a job as a waiter in a fancy Italian restaurant, and he has to perform for the customers. He doesn't know what the heck he's doing, but he starts singing some song about a man and a woman in a goofy made-up language that sounds like French, and Italian, and who knows what else.

Anyway, what I'm trying to say is that after all the times I've watched that restaurant scene, the words to Charlie's song still make no sense, but his singing and dancing still make me laugh. He got to Martha, Mom, and Dad, too. You should have heard them.

There we were, laughing on the couch, me with tears in my eyes I was howling so hard, when I realized that some things in life are just like Charlie's song. They make no sense, and no matter how hard you try to understand them they may never make sense, but they can still make you laugh. Or cry.

about the author

Marc Kornblatt worked as a waiter, bartender, doorman, typist, actor, and newspaper reporter before a friend who knew he was good with deadlines asked him to help her finish writing a book for young readers about World War II. He has since written other books for young readers about the Spanish Inquisition and the American Revolution, two picture books, and numerous stories and articles. *Understanding Buddy* is his first novel.

When not writing for children, Mr. Kornblatt writes plays, performs as a storyteller, and teaches Hebrew school. He lives in Madison, Wisconsin, with his wife, two children, and a retired greyhound racer named Gypsy.